CYNTHIA RYLANT

POPPLETON

IN FALL

BOOK SIX

Illustrated by
MARK TEAGUE

SCHOLASTIC INC.
New York Toronto London Auckland Sydney
Mexico City New Delhi Hong Kong

To Garen Thomas
C. R.

To Lynsey
M. T.

This book is being published simultaneously in hardcover by
the Blue Sky Press.

ISBN 0-590-84794-5

Text copyright © 1999 by Cynthia Rylant
Illustrations copyright © 1999 by Mark Teague
All rights reserved. Published by Scholastic Inc.

SCHOLASTIC and associated logos are trademarks
and/or registered trademarks of Scholastic Inc.

12 11 10 9 8 7 6 5 4 3 2 1   9/9 0/0 01 02 03 04

Printed in the United States of America   23

Design by Kathleen Westray

First Scholastic paperback printing, September 1999

CONTENTS

THE GEESE

One fall day
Poppleton saw two geese
flying south over his house.

"Hello, geese!" called Poppleton.

"Would you like some cookies?"

"Thanks!" said the geese,
and they landed.
Their names were Ted and Ned.

Poppleton enjoyed them very much
and was sad to see them go.
But soon after,
Poppleton saw five geese
flying south over his house.

"Hello, geese!" called Poppleton.
"Would you like some cookies?"
"You bet!" said the geese,
and they landed.
Their names were Mary, Sherry,
Harry, Larry, and Jerry.

They all knew Ted and Ned.

Poppleton enjoyed them very much
and was sad to see them go.
But soon after,
Poppleton saw eight geese
flying south over his house.

"Hello, geese!" Poppleton called.
"Would you like some cookies?"
(He hoped he had enough.)
"Would we ever!" said the geese,
and they landed.

Their names were Ann, Stan, Dan,
Fran, Han, Jan, Nan, and Van.

Poppleton enjoyed them very much
and was sad to see them go.

Because he was feeling
a little lonely, he went to visit
his neighbor Cherry Sue.

"Hello, Poppleton!" said Cherry Sue.
"What's new?"
"Too zoo moo poo boo coo do,"
said Poppleton.
"You'd better go take a nap,"
said Cherry Sue.

And he did.

THE COAT

The days were getting chilly.

Poppleton needed a new coat.

18

He went to see his friend Zacko
at the coat store.

"I need a new coat, Zacko,"
Poppleton said.

"Good!" said Zacko.

"Let me measure you."

Zacko measured
Poppleton from
head
to
toe.

Zacko measured
Poppleton from
side to side.

Zacko measured
Poppleton
all around.

Zacko shook his head.

"I have nothing to fit you,
Poppleton," said Zacko.

"Nothing to fit me?" cried Poppleton.
"You are too big," said Zacko.
"I am not!" cried Poppleton. And he
stormed out the door.

At home, Poppleton looked at himself
in the mirror.

He
looked
head
to
toe.

He looked side to side.

He looked
all around.

He got depressed.

Cherry Sue was walking by.

She saw Poppleton through the window.

"What's wrong, Poppleton?"

Cherry Sue asked.

"I am too big," said Poppleton glumly.

"Says who?" said Cherry Sue.

"Says Zacko," said Poppleton.

"Zacko's a ferret!" said Cherry Sue.

"I know that," said Poppleton.

"So of course he thinks you're too big!"
cried Cherry Sue.

"Did you tell him he's too small?"

"No," said Poppleton.

"Because you have good manners,"
said Cherry Sue.
"You are a big pig, Poppleton!" she said.
"Be proud!"

"I would like to be proud in a *coat*,"
said Poppleton.
"And Zacko has only small ones."
"Posh," said Cherry Sue. "Wait here."
She hurried home.

Soon she was back with a catalog.

Poppleton read the title:

BIG AND TALL PIGS.

"I get all the catalogs," said Cherry Sue.

"Even the ones for mice."

"Gee, thanks!" said Poppleton.

When the new coat arrived,
Poppleton slowly walked past
Zacko's store.
He looked very big.
He looked very proud.

But then he felt sorry for Zacko,
being so small.

So Poppleton went in and bought a scarf.

Each fall the Lions Club
had a pancake breakfast.
Poppleton loved this.
If anyone could make a pancake,
it was a lion.

So Poppleton invited Cherry Sue,
and they put on their Sunday clothes
and went to breakfast.

When they arrived, the lions
were flipping pancakes like crazy
and calling out, "Buckwheat! Cinnamon!
Johnnycake! Spicy nut! Apple! Banana!
Blueberry!"
"What flavor do you want, Cherry Sue?"
asked Poppleton.

"Plain," said Cherry Sue.

"Plain?" asked Poppleton. "You can make *plain* at home!"

"I like plain," said Cherry Sue.

"You probably like vanilla ice cream, too," said Poppleton.

"Love it," said Cherry Sue.

"All right. Wait here. I'll get you a
plain pancake," said Poppleton.
He went up to a lion.
"Are you making plain pancakes?"
Poppleton asked.

"ARE YOU KIDDING?" the lion roared.

"Sorry!" cried Poppleton, moving on.

He went up to another lion.

"Do you have any plain pancakes?" Poppleton asked.

"ARE YOU CRAZY?" the lion roared.

"Sorry!" cried Poppleton, moving on.

He went up to a third lion.

"Plain pancake, please,"
Poppleton said in a small voice.

"*NO!*" the lion roared.

Poppleton went back to Cherry Sue.

"Where's my pancake?" she asked.

"Try blueberry," said Poppleton.

"Why?" asked Cherry Sue.

"Just try blueberry," said Poppleton.

"Why?" asked Cherry Sue.

"JUST TRY BLUEBERRY!" yelled
Poppleton.

"WHY?" yelled Cherry Sue.

"BECAUSE THEY'RE GOING TO EAT ME
IF I ORDER PLAIN!" yelled Poppleton.

Cherry Sue thought.

"Blueberry will be perfect," she said.

And it was.

"You are a *perfect* friend,"
Poppleton said on the way home.
"I know," said Cherry Sue.

LIBRARY

LIBRARY